MAGIC HOOFBEATS

Fabulous Horse Tales

retold by *Josepha Sherman*

illustrated by *Linda Wingerter*

Barefoot Books
Celebrating Art and Story

Contents

Introduction

Once upon a time, there was a horse...

Picture that horse. See him running free, head high, mane flying in the wind and tail raised like a banner, or playing, dancing and leaping, hardly seeming to touch the ground. Is it any wonder that people down through the centuries have thought that the horse was a magical being?

The sight of the horse has caused some fantastic creatures to spring from the human imagination. Watching horses running so swiftly that they seemed to fly, the Greeks added wings to a mythical horse, and Pegasus, the flying horse, was born. Ride a horse, and you are taller than the tallest of men. Look too quickly at a rider on a horse and they merge into one being. And so the centaur, with the head and chest of a man and the body of a horse, was born. Glance too quickly at a horse, or mistake an antelope for a horse, and you might think the horse was horned. And so the unicorn, with its one horn, was born.

But even without all the fantastic reshapings added on by imagination, the horse remains a magical beast. Have you ever counted the number of white horses you see on one day? Or carefully turned a horseshoe in the shape of a 'U' so that the luck wouldn't run out? Some people believe that a horse's tooth will protect them from ill luck, or that a plait made from a grey stallion's hair will rid them of blemishes. No other animal has imprinted itself so thoroughly on the human mind and heart.

And no other animal but the horse has gathered so many wonderful folk tales about it.

This is a collection of horse folk tales from around the world, starring some very special animals — those that have their own magical powers. Note here that these horses, for all their magic, truly are horses. No folk tale in which the horse turns out at the end to be merely an enchanted human being was allowed into this book!

Welcome to the wonderful world of the magic horse.

North America

Pintos and the
Pawnee People

*T*he first horse, no bigger than a small dog, evolved in North America. But by the time people came to North America from Asia, somewhere between ten and thirty thousand years ago, there were no horses left in the New World. Where did they go? Many scientists say the horses may have migrated over the Bering Land Bridge (now sunk under the waters of the Bering Strait) into Asia, and that they journeyed from there into the Middle East and Europe. Others speculate that they may have died of disease while others believe the last North American horses may have been hunted into extinction by the first humans to settle in the New World.

On one fact all the scientists agree: when the Spanish came to the New World in the sixteenth century, looking for new lands to conquer and for goods to ship back to Europe, they brought their horses with them. Some of these horses escaped from their masters and raised their offspring in North America.

Until the return of the horse, the Pawnee people, like other nomadic Native American tribes, had been wandering on foot. It was a difficult life, since they couldn't cover enough ground to catch up with the grazing herds of buffalo or snare swifter game like the pronghorn antelope. But once the Pawnee had the horse, they could easily ride to fresh grazing lands and hunt enough meat to keep everyone in the tribe fed. Mounted on their swiftest steeds, Pawnee warriors could easily overtake a buffalo herd, and individual riders could dash into the herd, target just the buffalo they needed, and dash safely out again. The meat that they hunted in the summer months was cured and dried to provide food for the long, snowy winter season.

While the Pawnee didn't try breeding horses for speed or appearance, they did like 'flashy' horses such as pintos. Pintos are often piebald or skewbald, and favoured for their ability to blend in as well as for their speed and agility. The other breed that was popular among Native American tribes was the Appaloosa, a distinctive spotted breed that was most commonly found in the Pacific Northwest.

The Pawnee reservation is now a part of Oklahoma and there are less than seven hundred people who are part of the living nation. The Pawnee never cease telling stories about the days of old when their people and their horses were plentiful. The story of Lone Boy is one such tale.

Lone Boy and the Old Dun Horse
Pawnee — North American

Once, in the long-ago days when the Pawnee wandered freely over the plains, there lived an orphan named Lone Boy. He was the poorest in the tribe. He ate only what others did not want and wore only what others threw away. Everyone else in the tribe packed up their fine belongings, herded together their sleek horses, and rode on from one place to another. Lone Boy owned no horses and had to walk wearily after the tribe whenever they moved.

As he was walking after the tribe one day, Lone Boy heard a feeble whinny. He hurried down into a small ravine. There he found the saddest, oldest dun horse he had ever seen. Every rib showed on the skinny body, and its mane and tail looked like bits of tangled yarn.

'Poor old horse!' Lone Boy said. 'I'll take care of you.'

Everyone in the tribe laughed at him for bothering with such a sad-looking animal. But Lone Boy took good care of that horse. He fed it on the best grass he could find, and groomed it well.

One day, the tribe's scouts came hurrying back. They had found a large herd of buffalo — and one of the buffalo was a spotted calf. The hide of a spotted buffalo was powerful medicine indeed!

'Whoever brings me the spotted hide,' cried the head chief, 'will wed my daughter.'

Off raced all the hunters on their swift horses. Dreaming of the chief's beautiful daughter, Lone Boy went too, mounted on his old dun horse which ambled wearily along. The other hunters laughed at this, and left Lone Boy far behind.

When the hunters were all out of sight, the old horse stopped. 'Don't worry,' he said.

Lone Boy gasped. 'You — you spoke!'

'Don't be afraid of me, either. Come, cover me with this nice, cool mud. That's right, plaster it all over me. Give me the strength of the earth. Now, wait till we hear the hunters' call.'

The call came. The old dun horse shot forwards like the wind itself, far ahead of the other hunters. Again and again he dived into the buffalo herd. Again and again Lone Boy used his bow. The spotted calf fell to his arrows, and so did a fat buffalo cow.

'You have enough meat here,' the old dun horse said.

Lone Boy agreed. He took the hides and meat before any of the other hunters could see him, and the old dun horse carried it all with ease. Lone Boy gave the other poor people of the tribe all the meat they could eat. Then he took the magical spotted hide to the head chief.

The head chief's daughter smiled at Lone Boy. But the head chief would not let her wed a boy who owned nothing but one old horse.

'She will marry only a true hero,' he said.

'Never mind,' the old horse whispered to Lone Boy. 'You will prove yourself a true hero. Take back the spotted buffalo hide and wait.'

The next day, the tribe was attacked by an enemy war party. Lone Boy rode out with the others to defend his people.

'Charge the enemy only four times,' the dun horse warned.

Lone Boy charged the enemy. Each time, the arrows flew till they darkened the sky, but Lone Boy was unhurt. Each time he rode, he counted *coup*, striking down enemy warriors. This was

recognised by the tribe as a deed of courage. He did this once, twice, thrice, four times.

But the battle was not over. 'I rode four times without harm,' Lone Boy told himself. 'I will make just one more charge.'

He rode into the battle a fifth time, but an arrow struck down the old dun horse.

The battle ended. The tribe celebrated their victory. Lone Boy alone could not celebrate.

'If only I had obeyed you!' he mourned over the old horse's body. 'You would still be alive!'

Rain poured down, hiding the horse from Lone Boy's sight. When the storm finally ended, the old horse stirred, then scrambled to his feet.

'That was close,' he said. 'If you had not been so kind to me when you first found me, if you had not shared your meat with the poor people of the tribe, you never would have seen me again. But your good deeds were stronger than your disobedience, so here I am.'

The old horse swished his tail. 'It's time to get you your rightful place in the tribe. Each night for ten nights you must leave me on this hill. Do not come here until after the sun is up. If you disobey this time, you will lose everything.'

Each day, Lone Boy waited until the sun was shining before he climbed the hill. Each day, he found a different shining horse, bay or grey, black or gold, waiting for him, standing beside the old dun horse.

At the end of the ten days, Lone Boy placed the spotted buffalo hide on the old dun horse. He rode to the lodge of the head chief, his herd of shining horses trotting after him.

What could the head chief do? Lone Boy had won the spotted buffalo hide and proved himself a hero, and with such a fine, shining herd of horses, he was no longer poor.

So Lone Boy and the chief's daughter were wed, and lived happily together. And the old dun horse remained their treasured friend all their lives.

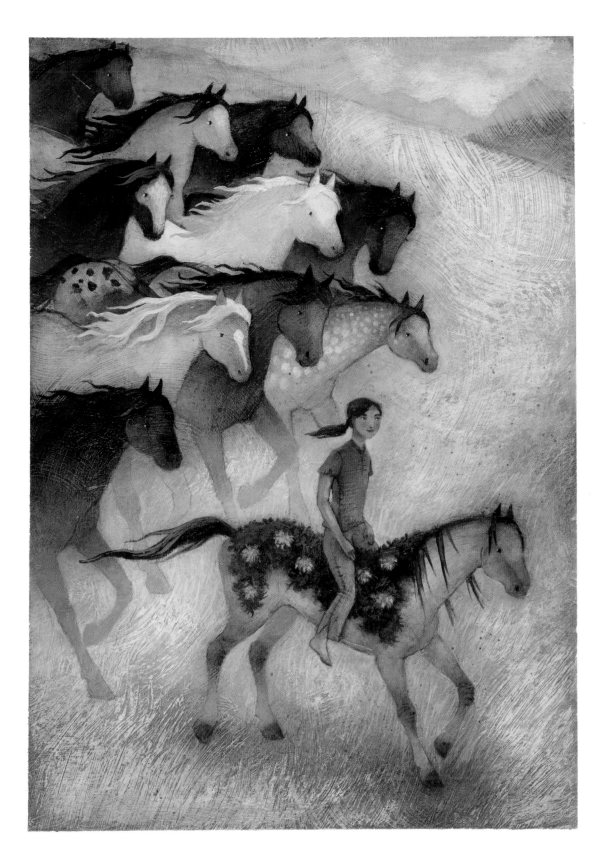

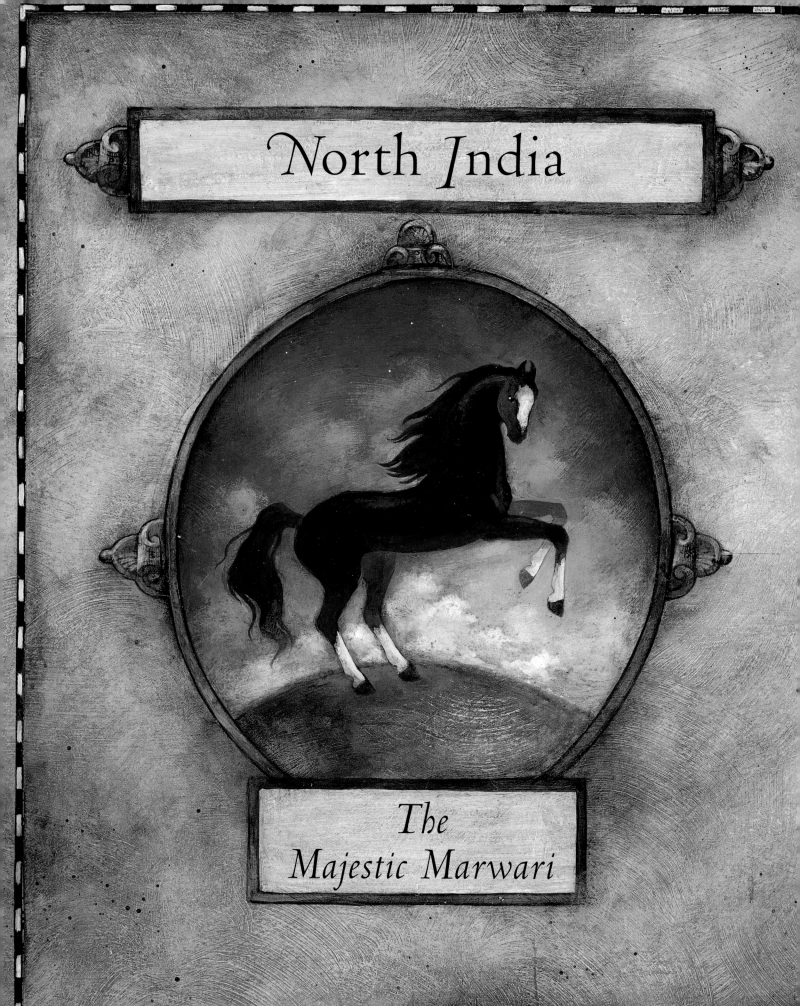

North India

The
Majestic Marwari

For many centuries, horses have played an important role in the northern states of modern-day India. The most notable breed in this part of the world is the Marwari Horse. The origins of the Marwari Horse are entwined with local folklore. According to the head priest of the monastery at Kalabar, a noted breeder of Marwari horses, the breed can be traced to a period 'when the ocean was churned to extract nectar for the Gods…a period when horses had wings'.

From the beginnings of time, the Marwari served the wealthy princes of India, and their courage earned them a reputation as fearless cavalry horses on the battlefield. The status of the Marwari as war-horses was unparalleled: they were even declared divine and were regarded as being superior to all men, including those of royal blood. Only the noble Rajput families and their warriors — the Kshatriyas — were permitted to ride them. When they went into battle with their masters, the Marwari were as ready as their riders to die in combat. If a Marwari horse's rider was victorious, the horse would carry him from the battlefield in triumph; if the rider was injured, he would carry him to safety; but if the rider was killed, the horse would lie down beside him and let himself be killed as well rather than abandoning his master.

The Marwari's sharp ears and excellent homing instinct can also help to save his rider's life. Marwari have exceptional hearing, so they can catch sounds from further away than most breeds, and so give their riders early warning of impending danger. Another advantage of the Marwari is their sturdiness: they are able to survive for extended periods of time without food or water in the hostile deserts of the north. If their riders get lost, these clever horses can often find their way safely home.

Marwari horses stand between 14 hands and 15.2 hands high. They have curvy rotating ears, a dignified bearing, and they are extremely intelligent and loyal companions. A properly trained Marwari can rise on his rear legs and land the front ones on the sides of an elephant, for his master to mount the elephant and engage in battle. When he leaps, he can span over three metres! He learns easily, is hardy and ever willing. All of these qualities are demonstrated in the next story, which is about a horse who knows his own worth, and knows better than the people around him how to handle the rebellion of a defiant local chieftain.

Terror

North Indian

Once, a horse-dealer from Gandhara set out with his horses for the royal city of Anga. The king was always watching for a hallowed horse for his young son, the crown prince.

What is a hallowed horse? It is a shining bay horse with a coat as smooth as the moonstone, a mane like the tossing of the waves, and wisdom far beyond belief. Whoever possessed such a hallowed horse would surely know joy.

And whoever sold such a horse to the king, the horse-dealer thought, would surely know wealth! Of course, he had no such horse, but his mares had foals, and who knew what foals might grow to be?

One foal he ignored. That was a fierce little creature who, even though he was a bay, as a hallowed horse was said to be, bit and kicked everyone. The horse-dealer named this hot-tempered foal Terror.

'I will sell Terror to the first man foolish enough to buy him!'

A potter saw Terror and said, 'What a pretty little horse!'

Terror hurried to the potter and began to lick and nuzzle him.

'What a sweet little horse!' the potter said. 'What is his name?'

'Terror,' the horse-dealer told him, but hurried to add, 'it's a joke.' As it happened, the horse-dealer owed the potter money, so he said, 'Why not take this horse in exchange for what I owe you?'

The little horse licked the potter on the cheek. 'Done,' said the potter.

He took Terror home, and he and his wife kept the little horse as their pet.

The years passed, and the foal grew into a fine bay horse.

Meanwhile, in the royal court at Anga, the king died, and his son, the young crown prince, took the throne at the age of twelve.

The chieftains who had owed allegiance to the old king did not like the idea of owing allegiance to such a young king.

'We won't pay tribute to that little boy!' shouted Rajah Ganesha, the head of the rebellious chieftains. 'Let us wait till he goes hunting all alone. Then we shall capture him and I shall be your king!'

Whispers of rebellion reached the ears of the prime minister. He said to the young king, 'Sire, you must not leave the palace grounds until we find you a hallowed horse that will keep you safe.'

'Must I be a prisoner?' the young king retorted. 'Must I stay indoors till you find a horse that probably doesn't even exist?'

The prime minister quickly called for all the horse-dealers in the land. Among them was the one who had given Terror to the potter. 'I did have a bay horse such as you describe,' he said slowly, 'but it was a mean-spirited beast, and so I gave it away to a potter.'

The prime minister and his retinue went to the potter.

'What have you done with the horse the horse-dealer gave you?'

The potter blinked in surprise. 'Why, it is well, quite well. Now that it is grown, my little Terror carries my sacks of clay quite nicely.'

'We will buy Terror from you for a sack of gold.'

'No! I like my horse.'

'Two sacks of gold!'

'No!'

'Don't be a fool,' a voice whispered in the potter's ear. 'This is your chance for wealth.'

The potter thought it was his wife's whisper. 'How can a man sell his horse — a horse that is like a son to me?'

'You are making me angry!' the voice whispered. 'If your son was destined to be prime minister, would you force him to stay a potter? Tell them, "I will take only the price of a hallowed horse." And you will get not two but a dozen sacks of gold!'

Just then, the potter's wife walked by. Then who had been whispering in his ear? He turned, and saw Terror staring back at him. 'You...'

'Do as I say!' Terror commanded.

So the potter told the prime minister, 'Give me the price of a hallowed horse.'

He was given a dozen sacks of gold, enough to make him a wealthy man.

Terror went off with the prime minister and was given a fine stall, with plenty of soft straw for his bed and the finest oats and hay.

But Terror refused to eat.

'He wishes to be honoured like a true hallowed horse,' the wise men decided, so they asked musicians to play for him.

Terror still refused to eat.

'We have not honoured him enough,' the wise men decided. 'He still does not feel at home.'

So they took out the old wooden manger, and put in one of shining gold.

Terror still refused to eat.

The wise men consulted their books and scrolls. 'Ah! We know what the hallowed horse wants! He must be coaxed to eat by the first lady of all the land.'

'That would be the king's wife — if only the king had a wife!'

'His cousin!' the wise men decided. 'His little first cousin is his closest kin — we must find her!'

Off the wise men hurried, searching here and hunting there. At last the little girl was found, sitting in a mango tree munching the fruit. 'I don't want to come down!' she said. 'I like it up here. Though I wish I had some sweets, too.'

'We will give you sweets. We will give you anything you want. But first you must feed the hallowed horse.'

Off she went to Terror's stall. Terror refused even to sniff at her. The girl said, 'I am the king's first cousin, so they call me first lady.

19

Of course, once he's married, I won't be much of anybody.'

Terror tossed his mane and snorted.

'I know you're called Terror,' the girl continued. 'I'm called Candy-Cheek because I like sweets and candy so much. I suppose it's silly to think that a horse can talk. But at least you can listen. I was hiding in a tree because terrible things are happening. Rajah Ganesha is leading an army of rebels against us. He wants to marry me. And he wants to cut off the prime minister's head, then capture my cousin, the king, and leave him on a desert island to die of starvation.'

She frowned at Terror. 'That's right. And here you are, with plenty to eat — and yet you're trying to die of starvation, too!'

'For your sake,' Terror said, 'I will eat.'

'You can talk! Oh, wonderful! Eat and grow strong, and then you can go and bite off Rajah Ganesha's ear to teach him a lesson!'

'I shall teach him a lesson right now,' Terror said. 'Open the stall door.'

'Not without me!' Candy-Cheek said bravely. 'I want to go with you.'

'Very well. Open the door and jump on my back — then hold fast!'

Candy-Cheek jumped on Terror's back, and he raced off like the wind itself, straight to the rebel camp. There he stopped short and gave a great neigh. Every horse in the camp neighed back, saying in horse language, 'This is our leader!'

Rajah Ganesha came running. 'Look at this!' he cried to his men. 'My child bride has come to me.'

But Terror gave a second commanding neigh, and all the horses in the camp turned on their riders, caught them by their belts, and carried them off. Terror lunged forwards and bit off Rajah Ganesha's ear, then led the charge back to the city. There, the royal army quickly put an end to the rebellion.

That evening, everyone in Anga celebrated.

'Long live our king!' they cried.

'Long live our brave Candy-Cheek!'

'And long live the wonder horse, the hallowed horse, Terror!'

The Basque Country

The
Pottock Pony

*T*he Basque region is a rugged, mountainous area stretching from southwest France across the Pyrenees to northern Spain. This area of Europe is famous for the Pottock — an ancient breed of small horse which can also be found, with just slight variations, in Poland, Portugal and Spain.

Although no one is sure of the true origins of the Pottock, this friendly and hardworking mountain pony is probably a direct descendant of the prehistoric horses which are represented on the cave wall drawings of Lascaux, Combarelles and Isturitz in France, and Altamira in Spain. Nowadays, Pottock ponies are brown and black, and some scientists believe that they took on this colouring after the last ice age, when warmer weather and higher rainfall led to the growth of richer vegetation and forests. These camouflage colours will have helped the horses to escape predators.

In later centuries, Pottock ponies became an indispensable part of traditional Basque life, working underground in the mountain mines, and above ground as pack animals, helping to transport goods to and fro across the mountains. Small, stocky and even-tempered, they were easy to train and dependable to work with. However, as the mountain regions became steadily more populated with small farming communities and villages, the ponies were driven into more barren areas higher up in the hills. As recently as the 1950s, groups of wild ponies could be found running free in isolated mountain areas. Nowadays, they are rounded up once a year, in early January, branded, and either released again or sold on as breeding stock. Since the late 1970s, they have been in increasing demand as riding animals, and their calm nature and small size has made them very popular as mounts for children. Pottock ponies also perform well as show jumpers, in the dressage arena, and in harness.

Some believe that the Pottock ponies were taken to the New World by Spanish navigators during the sixteenth and seventeenth centuries. If this is the case, the Pottock are at least in part the ancestors of the horses of North America.

Since horses have been such a valuable asset to the Basque people for centuries beyond telling, it is no surprise that a magical white mare becomes the protectress of the heroine in this folk tale. A white horse will have been a rarity among the Pottock, so the fact that this mare is white gives her a numinous and other-worldly quality.

The White Mare
Basque

Once there lived a king with three daughters. The youngest was named Fifine, and she was his favourite since she was kind and good of heart.

Now, one day the king was sitting peacefully with his daughters when he felt something tickle his ear. 'What's this?' he cried.

Fifine looked and pounced. 'A flea!' she said, holding it between her thumb and forefinger. 'But it's larger than any normal flea.'

Sure enough, it was. Curious, the king had it put in a container so that it could be studied. But the flea grew so swiftly that it quickly outgrew the container. The king had it placed in a barrel. But the flea grew swiftly. The flea grew so swiftly that it quickly outgrew the barrel. It was now as large as a cow!

'That's large enough!' the king decided. He had the flea slain and its skin tanned, just as though it really had been a cow. And, since he had a fanciful turn of mind, the king issued a proclamation: whoever could name the animal that had provided this skin should have one of the three princesses as his bride.

Of course, the king never expected anyone to be able to guess. For long and long again, no would-be suitor succeeded. But one day a prince arrived, a fine fellow in shining golden armour. 'Your Majesty,' he said, 'that is the skin of a flea grown in a barrel.'

So it was. The king, relieved that the winner of the contest should be a prince, and a Golden Prince at that, told him to step forth and pick one of the three princesses for his bride.

'So I shall,' the Golden Prince agreed, 'in two days.'

The entire royal palace was in a stir, as can be imagined.

Everyone wanted to prepare as fine a feast for the Golden Prince as ever had been seen. Only Fifine wasn't happy. She went down to the royal stables, to the stall of her favourite horse, the White Mare.

'Be wary,' the White Mare warned her. 'That is not truly a prince, but an evil spirit — and it is you he intends to choose.'

'I must warn my father!'

'He will not believe you. No one in the entire palace will believe you! The Golden Prince will see to that. And once the Golden Prince has chosen you, we shall never be free.'

'What can I do?'

'Listen to me and heed my words. Your father will wish to give you a fine wedding present. Refuse anything he offers. Tell him that you want nothing but the White Mare. You must not leave the palace without me — and you must be riding me when you go.'

Fifine left the stable with a heart full of grief. She borrowed ugly clothes from a servant and went to meet the Golden Prince with her hair dirty and full of ashes. But he only smiled. 'I choose you, Princess Fifine, for my bride.'

Everyone rejoiced — everyone but Fifine. Sure enough, after the feast, her father said, 'Come, my dear. I will give you a fine wedding present.'

'I want only the White Mare,' she replied.

'What, a mangy old horse? Nonsense! I will give you fifty bags of gold.'

'All I want is the White Mare.'

'You cannot have the White Mare!' the king exclaimed. 'She belonged to your poor dead mother. I will not let the White Mare go.'

'Then the Golden Prince may not wed me. I will not leave here unless I may leave riding the White Mare.'

What could her father do? He didn't want to lose so fine and shining a son-in-law. At last he muttered, 'Very well, you may have the White Mare.'

The Golden Prince frowned. 'This is such an ugly horse! We shall tie it behind my carriage so that no one can see it.'

But Fifine remembered the White Mare's warning. 'Oh, that won't do. My White Mare is so swift that she can outrun all your carriage horses. We shall ride on in front, and you shall follow.'

With that, Fifine threw herself on to the White Mare's back, and the White Mare sped off like lightning. The Golden Prince swore an angry oath and whipped his carriage horses after them.

'White Mare, White Mare, they're gaining!' Fifine gasped.

'Not for long,' the White Mare replied. She stopped short and struck the earth three times with a hoof, so strongly that the earth rang. And a great abyss opened before her.

'Enter, evil one!' the White Mare cried. 'Enter and stay for seven years.'

With that, the carriage, Golden Prince and all, flew down into the abyss, and the earth closed over them.

'We're safe!' Fifine gasped.

'For only seven years,' the White Mare corrected her. 'I could not provide you with safety for ever.' She sighed. 'The world is a wide and dangerous place for a pretty young princess alone, so I shall disguise you as a young prince.'

This sounded splendid to Fifine, who had never seen the wide world beyond the palace. She travelled on in her magical disguise, her only companion the White Mare, and many sights both good and ill did she see.

At last, weary from their journeying, they came to a great palace. 'This is a good place for us to stop,' the White Mare said. 'The queen who rules has a son who is as kind as he is handsome. But you must not tell anyone yet that you are anything but a prince.'

The queen and her son made
Fifine and her White Mare welcome.
Fifine liked him from the first, but
she remembered the White Mare's
warning and said nothing of her
true identity.

Several weeks passed, and one day the
prince told his mother, 'I had the strangest
dream. I dreamed that our visitor was
a princess!'

'How odd!' the queen exclaimed.
'Let us test this. Take our guest
to the market. If he is really
she, our guest will surely stop
at the jewellery stall.'

But Fifine, guessing at the trick,
passed right by the jewellery stall
and went straight to the stall selling
knives and swords.

That night, the prince once more dreamed that their guest was a princess.

'We shall try a bit of magic,' the queen told him. She knew just one small spell.
'Take our guest to the orchard. If this truly is a girl, the apple blossoms will
fall on her.'

But as the apple blossoms fell, the White Mare blew them aside. They all landed
on the prince!

'So much for magic,' the queen laughed.

That night, she slipped into the guest room where Fifine slept. And she caught
Fifine asleep in a silken gown.

'So you are a princess!' the queen cried. 'How clever you were to keep yourself
disguised! But you are safe here.'

In the days that followed, the prince and princess walked together and talked together. They fell in love. And at last, they married.

'This is as it should be,' the White Mare said. 'You will not need me for seven years. But you must always keep this magic flute with you. When danger arises, play it, and I will come to you.' With that, the White Mare galloped away.

For seven years, Fifine and her husband lived happily together, and had two children, whom they loved dearly.

But one day the prince had to leave on a royal journey. Since their children were still too young to travel, Fifine stayed behind. She was with them in the palace garden when the earth shook and tore itself open. Up rose the Golden Prince, free after his seven years' imprisonment.

'Come with me, Fifine,' he snarled, 'or I shall slay your children!'

Fifine hugged her children to her. 'You shall not hurt them! But before I go with you, first you must let me play a little farewell tune on my flute.'

The Golden Prince shrugged. 'If it is brief.'

Indeed, it was. For with the very first note, the White Mare came galloping into the garden, fire blazing from her eyes. 'I did not know the right magic seven years ago,' she cried. 'But after seven years, I have learned it!'

Before the Golden Prince could say a word, the White Mare stamped on the ground, once, twice, thrice, three mighty blows that shook the earth.

'Earth,' the White Mare cried, 'here is evil! Earth, swallow him up! Earth, keep him for ever!'

The earth tore open under the Golden Prince's feet. Shouting with rage, he fell into the pit. Without a sound, the earth closed once more — and the Golden Prince was never seen again.

'Now you are truly safe,' the White Mare told Fifine. 'And I may at last go home!'

She stamped her foot, and a beautiful fountain sprang up. As Fifine and her children marvelled at it, the White Mare leaped up into the air and flew away.

Fifine's husband soon came home from his journey. The family lived long and happily. And they never forgot the White Mare.

Russia

Horses of the Steppes

*H*orses have been a part of everyday life in Russia for over six thousand years. Without them, it would have been impossible for people to colonise the wild Russian steppes and forests, or for the Russian army to operate effectively in the era before the development of military hardware. Horses also played a vital role in long-distance communications, pulling sleighs and troikas with news and with goods from one part of the country to another. In addition, Russians have long enjoyed horseracing, especially trotting races, and other equestrian sports, with games such as *chavgan* (a form of polo) and *supramakh* (a kind of basketball played on horseback) being extremely popular in the lands around the Caucasus mountains.

Russians have always had a deep affection for their horses. Stories abound of incidents in which people have been saved by their dear troika hacks or their brave mounts. The Don — a type of Russian steppe horse — can guide its rider to safety through a snow blizzard or the densest of fogs. From the Don, the Budenny was later bred as a speedy and robust cavalry horse. In the mountain regions, many people owe their lives to the sure-footed and intrepid Kabardin — a mountain horse known for its incredible endurance over long distances.

One of the most famous of Russian breeds is the Orlov, which was developed by a wealthy Russian aristocrat, Count Orlov, as a trotter during the eighteenth century. A small, neat horse with a long stride, the Orlov trotter can hold its pace over considerable distances and this, combined with its handsome physique and bold character, has earned it pride of place in Russian folklore and literature.

The breeds that evolved in the harsh climate of the Russian steppes needed to be able to endure extreme conditions, and to find sustenance deep beneath the frost and snow of winter. The Bashkir, a tough steppe and mountain pony, is one of the hardiest breeds in the world. Bashkirs are usually chestnut coloured, with thick, curly winter coats that can be spun to make cloth. They can fend for themselves in sub-zero conditions, and can work day after day without needing supplementary food.

The little humpbacked horse in the next story is likely to be a Bashkir. He is playful, intelligent and resourceful, and shows everyone that horses should not be judged just on appearance.

The Little Humpbacked Horse
Russian

Once, in the days when a tsar ruled Russia, there lived a farmer with three sons: Danilo, Gavrilo and Ivan. Now, Ivan was a kind, gentle young man, but his older brothers, who were cold and sharp as ice, called him Ivan the Fool.

One morning, the farmer went out to his fields. How terrible! A thief had come during the night and stolen some hay.

'I will catch the thief,' Danilo boasted.

That night, he sat waiting in the field. But the night was cold.

'Why should I freeze just to save some hay?' Danilo asked. Finding a warm corner of the barn, he fell asleep.

In the morning, the farmer found that more of his hay had been stolen. Danilo only shrugged. 'I did my best to scare the thief away.'

Nor did Gavrilo fare any better the second night. He, too, fell asleep and let the thief steal hay.

'Now it is my turn!' Ivan exclaimed.

'What, you?' his brothers laughed. 'Foolish Ivan? What can you do that we could not?'

He could stay awake and on guard, Ivan told himself. Hugging his arms against the cold, Ivan patrolled back and forth through the field. All at once he saw the thief — a beautiful mare so white she blazed like the moon, with a mane and tail like burning gold. Ivan waited…waited…then jumped! He landed on the mare's back — but he landed backwards, facing her tail! The mare leapt straight up in the air, and Ivan clung to that tail with all his might. He clung as she bucked and kicked, and at last raced off like a comet into the night. No matter what the mare did, Ivan stuck to her back.

At last the mare, panting and shuddering, returned to the field and stopped. 'You have won,' she said. 'Keep me in your barn for three days, Ivan, but let no one see me. Each dawn let me out to roll in the morning dew. At the end of the three days, give me my freedom, and I shall leave you a wondrous reward.'

Ivan did as the white mare bade, hiding her away, then staggered wearily home. When his father asked him if he'd seen the thief, Ivan said with a tired laugh, 'I not only saw the thief, I rode that thief near and far and near again, and you can believe that I am truly weary.'

His father didn't believe him, not with Danilo and Gavrilo there to jeer. Ivan didn't care. He went straight to sleep.

Three days passed. Each dawn, he let the white mare roll in the morning dew. And on the morning of the fourth day, he let her go. The white mare soared off, swift as a comet, and Ivan sighed and turned to the barn.

Sure enough, here was the wonder she had promised. Two beautiful stallions pranced there, one a rich, gleaming brown, the other a soft, glowing grey, their manes and tails burning like gold.

A third horse peeped out of the barn. He was a tiny fellow, no bigger than a pony. His back was humped, his ears were long and floppy, but his eyes were bright and clever. Ivan groomed and pampered the two beautiful stallions, but he quickly came to love the little humpbacked horse, who played with him like a dog, clapping his long ears together for joy.

But two shining stallions cannot be kept a secret for long. Danilo and Gavrilo, spying on their brother, saw the horses. 'Why should it be our fool of a brother who owns such splendid steeds? We could sell those horses to the tsar himself!'

That night, Danilo and Gavrilo stole the two shining stallions, and off they went to the great fair that was held in the tsar's royal city.

The morning came, and Ivan went to the barn. The little humpbacked horse greeted him with joy, bouncing about and clapping his long ears together.

'Where are the two shining stallions?' Ivan cried.

'Your brothers have stolen them. Ah, don't look so sad! We can overtake them with ease.' The little horse trotted forward. 'Come, sit on my back. Don't worry! You won't harm me. Sit tight and hold fast to my ears.'

Wondering, Ivan sat on the little horse's back and took a firm grip on the long ears. The little horse shot forward like an arrow from a bow. So fast did he speed that in less time than it took Ivan to catch his breath, they had overtaken Danilo and Gavrilo and the two shining stallions.

'Where are you taking my horses?' Ivan cried.

Danilo and Gavrilo were astonished to see their brother had caught up with them. They laughed to see him riding so ridiculous a horse. But they said, hanging their heads, 'We did not want to steal from you. But you are very selfish, brother. Our poor parents struggle to feed us all, yet you hide these splendid steeds that could fetch a fine price at the tsar's fair.'

'True enough,' Ivan admitted. 'But since the horses are mine, I will go with you to sell them.'

Danilo and Gavrilo frowned. They did not want Ivan with them. But they nodded. Off they all went to the royal fair.

Sure enough, there was the tsar himself, a cruel, foolish old man. He saw the two shining stallions and at once wished to buy them, paying Ivan with two sacks of gold. Ivan told his brothers, 'Take this gold to our parents.'

Danilo and Gavrilo went home.

Meanwhile, the royal grooms tried to lead away the two shining stallions. But the

stallions bucked and kicked and refused to be led. 'Stop that!' Ivan said to the horses. 'Mind your manners.'

He took them by the halters — and at once the horses became mild as lambs. The tsar saw this, and told Ivan, 'You are my new head groom.'

That did not sit well with the other grooms. They spied on Ivan and saw him talking over his sudden good fortune with the little humpbacked horse. Then the grooms went straight to the tsar and lied:

'Your new head groom is a sorcerer! He claimed that he could capture the Golden Pig with the Silver Tusks. But he refused to give that prize to you.'

'Bring Ivan to me!' the tsar thundered.

So Ivan was dragged before the tsar, who ordered, 'Bring me the Golden Pig with the Silver Tusks, and do it within seven days — or you shall die!'

Ivan went sadly back to the stables, where the little humpbacked horse asked, 'What is wrong?'

'I must bring the tsar the Golden Pig with the Silver Tusks within seven days,' Ivan replied, 'or I will die.'

'That is not such a terrible task,' the little horse said. 'I shall help you. Go to the tsar and tell him that you must have a bucket of golden corn, a bucket of silver wheat, and a rope of strongest silk.'

Ivan did just that. When the little humpbacked horse breathed over them, the buckets and rope fitted into a small saddlebag. Ivan and the little humpbacked horse set out on their journey. The little horse ran like the wind, soared like the eagle, and soon they were in the Land of the South, in the valley of the Golden Pig with the Silver Tusks.

'The Golden Pig has twelve sucklings,' the little horse told Ivan. 'We must catch them all.' Following the little horse's advice, Ivan placed the golden corn at one end of the valley, the silver wheat at the other. The Golden Pig came running, gleaming in the sun, to eat the golden corn. Her twelve sucklings hurried to eat the silver wheat. Ivan caught the baby pigs one by one, tying them to his saddle with the strong, silken rope. He leapt on to the little humpbacked horse and they began to race back to the tsar's court.

As soon as the Golden Pig with the Silver Tusks saw that her sucklings were being carried away, she raced after them, right into the royal palace.

'Here they are,' Ivan cried to the tsar. 'I've brought you the Golden Pig with the Silver Tusks, and all her sucklings as well!'

And he went wearily off to the stables to rest.

Now even the boyars — the nobles — were jealous of this amazing new head groom. 'This was but a joke to him,' they whispered to the tsar. 'If he were truly loyal to you, he would bring you the Mare with the Seven Manes.'

So the tsar ordered Ivan to bring him the Mare with the Seven Manes, and do it within seven days, or die a horrible death.

'This is not such a terrible task,' the little humpbacked horse told Ivan. 'This time we shall need a stone stable with one entrance and one exit. We must take with us a horsehide and a heavy iron hammer.'

Ivan obeyed, ordering that a stone stable be built and that he be given the horsehide and the iron hammer. The little humpbacked horse breathed on the hide and the hammer, and they fitted into a saddlebag. Off the little horse flew with Ivan to a vast green meadow.

'Here is where the Mare with the Seven Manes grazes,' the little horse said. 'She and her seven fiery sons. Sew me into the horsehide and be ready with the iron hammer.'

When the Mare with the Seven Manes saw another horse in her meadow, she charged, screaming with rage. As she tore the horsehide from the little humpbacked horse, Ivan sprang from hiding and hit her between the ears with the iron hammer. It was a blow that would have slain an ordinary horse, but it merely stunned the Mare with the Seven Manes. She let Ivan lead her back to the tsar's palace, and her seven sons followed, right into the stone stable. The entrance was shut behind them, and Ivan and the little humpbacked horse rode safely out of the exit, barring it behind them.

'The horses are yours,' Ivan told the tsar.

Now the boyars were truly worried. How could they ever be rid of this troublesome head groom?

So they went to the tsar and said, 'Capturing the Pig and the Mare were mere jests for Ivan. Let him show his loyalty by a true test. Ask him to bring you the beautiful Princess of the Golden Boat, she whom you've long wished to wed.'

The Princess of the Golden Boat had refused the tsar. Remembering this, the tsar thundered at Ivan, 'Bring me the Princess of the Golden Boat, and do it within seven days, or you shall die!'

Ivan trudged sadly back to the stables. When the little humpbacked horse heard what was wrong, he said, 'This is still not such a terrible task. This time you must ask for two gold-embroidered scarves, a lovely silken tent, and all the trappings of a royal feast.'

The little horse breathed on them. Ivan placed them in the saddlebag, and they rode and flew, flew and rode, to the sea at the edge of the world.

'Here you must pitch the tent,' the little horse said. 'Spread out the scarves and set out the feast on them. Then hide behind the tent and wait. The Princess of the Golden Boat will come ashore and enter the tent to see what lies within. Then you must seize her and call for me.'

Ivan did as he was told. Here came the Princess of the Golden Boat, which was rowed with magic silver oars. The boat came to shore, and the princess entered the tent.

Ivan was struck with love from his first sight of her. Instead of seizing her, he could do nothing but stare in wonder. The princess tasted some of the feast, and then sprang back into her golden boat. Soon the silver oars had rowed her out of sight.

The little humpbacked horse galloped up. 'What happened? What went wrong?'

'It was my fault,' Ivan said. 'I saw her, loved her, and failed to move. Now I shall never see her again.'

'Never mind, never mind,' the little horse said. 'She will surely come again. But if you fail this time, there will be nothing for you but to let the tsar put you to death.'

The new day came. The Princess of the Golden Boat did come to see the mysterious tent once more. This time Ivan didn't hesitate. He sprang from hiding and seized her — and when the princess saw what a handsome young man he was, she forgot to struggle.

'I can't take you back,' Ivan told her. 'The tsar wishes to wed you.'

'I must go with you,' she said, 'or the tsar will kill you!'

'You shall return,' the little humpbacked horse told them both, 'and all will be well.'

They rode back to the tsar's palace. He was full of joy to see the lovely Princess of the Golden Boat there in his court, and told her, 'You will make a most wonderful bride!'

'Not for you!' she snapped. 'You are too old and ugly and cruel. Only if you grow young and handsome and kind, will I wed you.'

'How can that happen?' the tsar asked.

'You must place three great cauldrons in the courtyard. The first must be filled with scalding mare's milk, the second with boiling water, and the third with cold water. He who is brave enough to bathe for one minute in the first cauldron, two minutes in the second and three minutes in the third will instantly become so splendid a man that it can scarcely be believed. I will wed whatever man will undergo such a test.'

The tsar was filled with fright. Who could possibly survive such a test? 'Send for my head groom!' he commanded.

When Ivan was brought before him, the tsar ordered, 'You shall bathe in three cauldrons, one of cold water, one of boiling water, and one of scalding mare's milk.'

The tsar thought that if Ivan could survive, so could he. And if Ivan should not survive, well then, the tsar would be rid of this stranger who could solve every problem and might someday grow too powerful!

Terrified, Ivan went back to the stables. When the little humpbacked horse asked what was wrong, Ivan told him bitterly, 'I am to be treated like any chicken or pig, and prepared for dinner. The tsar means to boil me to death.'

'Weep not, my friend,' the little horse said soothingly. 'Now at last I may perform a true service for you. When you go to face the three cauldrons, insist that you have a chance to bid me farewell then and there. I shall gallop three times about the cauldrons, then dip my nose into each and sprinkle you. Once I have done so, don't hesitate a moment, but leap into each cauldron in turn. Trust in me and all will be well.'

No sooner had he finished speaking than the guards came to bring Ivan before the tsar and all the courtiers. There stood the three cauldrons, two of them boiling fiercely. 'Bathe!' the tsar commanded.

'First let me say farewell to my little humpbacked horse,' Ivan said. 'He has been almost a brother to me.'

Here came the little humpbacked horse, playing and prancing like a foal, clapping his long ears together happily. He burst into a gallop, racing about the three cauldrons once, twice, thrice, dipping his nose into each and sprinkling his master.

No sooner had the little humpbacked horse finished than Ivan leapt boldly into the first cauldron, filled with scalding mare's milk — and was not harmed. He leapt into the second cauldron, filled with boiling water — and was not harmed. He leaped into the third cauldron, filled with cold water — and if he had gone into it a good-looking fellow, he rose out of it a true, regal prince, so splendid that even the boyars began to bow to him.

'You shall not have all the magic!' the tsar cried.

Without another word, he hurled himself into the cauldron of scalding mare's milk. But there was no little humpbacked horse to shield him. And in an instant, that was the end of the tsar.

The Princess of the Golden Boat stepped forth. 'Your tsar would have made me his wife. But I will wed only the man who brought me here!'

Everyone cheered. 'Yes!' they cried. 'You two shall rule this land!'

Ivan and the Princess of the Golden Boat were wed that very day, and took their thrones. The little humpbacked horse stayed with them as their counsellor and friend. And so they ruled wisely, well and happily.

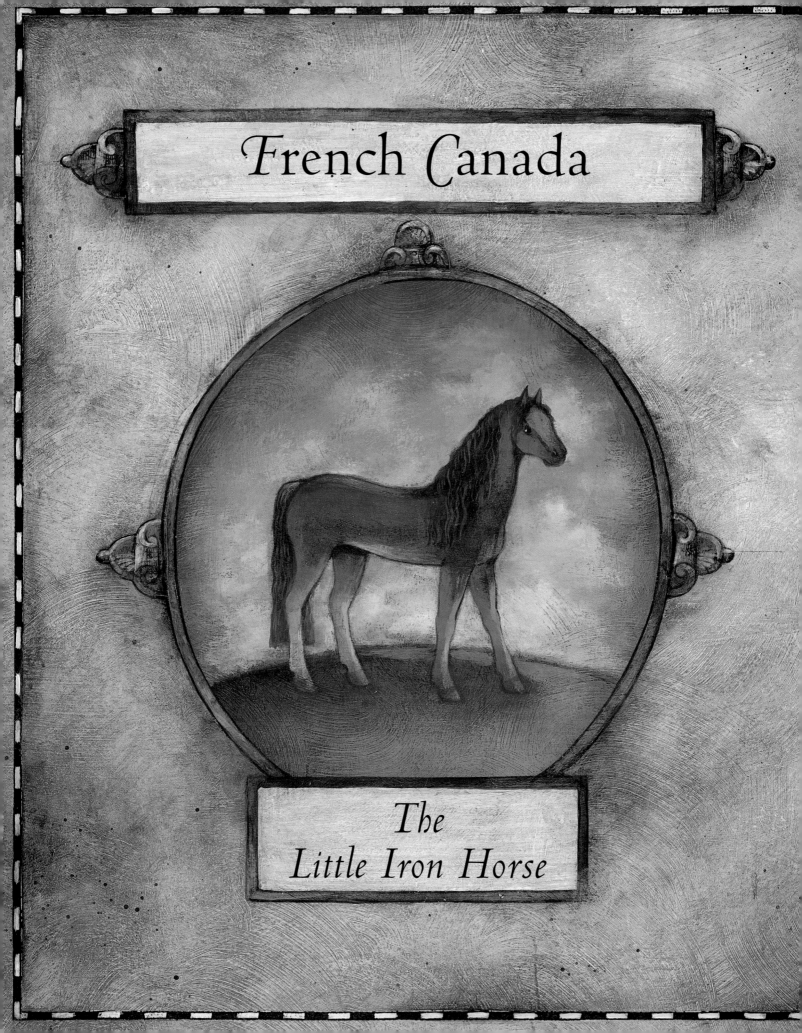

French Canada

The
Little Iron Horse

The horses of present-day French Canada are not native to the country; they are descended from French stallions and mares that were sent over in the seventeenth century by the French King, Louis XIV, to help the first settlers as they tried to carve out a living in the harsh climate of the St Lawrence River valley. Louis sent two breeds: Breton horses, which were small and strong, and Norman horses, which were similar to Bretons but with finer features, having both Spanish Barb and Arab blood. These two breeds each included several types, and were crossbred with one another by the French Canadian settlers. From them a variety of horses developed — some were heavy-built draught horses, others were trotters, with feathered legs and flowing manes and tails, and others again were pacers. Together, these types evolved over the centuries to create what is now known as the French Canadian horse.

In the years when Canada was being settled by pioneers from Europe, French Canadian horses were an essential part of life. They cleared and worked the land, pulled carriages and provided entertainment as racehorses. They were later used in battle in the American Civil War. By the mid nineteenth century, the number of French Canadian horses had dropped drastically. Even with a breeding programme set up by the federal government, there are now only a few thousand left. They are still highly valued for their strength, willingness to work hard, and for their adaptability.

Until the arrival of mechanised farming methods, the French Canadian horse had to endure many hardships — surviving sub-zero temperatures and heavy snows in winter, often with only straw to eat after many hours of hard labour, and then being plagued by mosquitoes and flies in summer. This hard life meant that the horses became smaller and tougher with each generation, and they soon earned themselves the nickname 'little iron horse'. Some of these strong, stoic and hard-working companions became legendary for their courage and stamina, and even today, French Canadians exchange stories of 'little iron horses' who have been able to work year in and year out in extreme conditions without showing any signs of exhaustion, while bigger and stronger horses have been worn to the bone. The next story fits well into this tradition, as the white horse that becomes Petit Jean's companion is easily able to outpace his black rival when his rider has to race for his life.

Petit Jean and the White Horse
French Canadian

Once there was an old man, a widower with only one son, a child called Petit Jean, Little John. Now the old man was a bitter sort, one who saw the whole world as his enemy. Since he didn't want to blame himself for his troubles, he blamed all that went wrong on his son, poor Petit Jean. The old man beat Petit Jean if the weather was too warm or the soup too cold. He beat that poor boy like a rug.

One day, Petit Jean made up his mind that he'd had enough of this. He ran away into the wide, wild world.

Wide and wild the world is indeed. Petit Jean followed a road until it became a path, and the path until it became nothing but forest all around him. The night was coming on, and the darkness and cold, and one long, long wolfish howl from the trees made Petit Jean shiver. Oh, he'd better find himself some shelter for the night!

Was that not the faintest glimmer of light up ahead? Petit Jean hurried forward, and all at once burst out of the forest into a clearing. There before him stood a stable and a tall tower. The closer he came to it, the darker that tower looked, as though no one had ever lived in it, save maybe a bat or two. Petit Jean would have turned and fled, but night was even darker than the tower, and he couldn't see so much as a hint of a path.

So…he knocked. Rap-rap-rap.

Nothing. He knocked again, with a little more force. Rap-rap-rap.

Still nothing. Petit Jean took a deep breath and knocked with all his force. RAP-RAP-RAP!

The door groaned open. There stood an old woman, staring at him with eyes like two black chips of stone. 'What's this?' she asked, her voice harsh as the croak of a raven. 'What's this? You are the first to knock at my door, boy, in a hundred years!'

Petit Jean wanted to run away. But once upon a time — so long ago it seemed! — his mother had told him always to be polite. So he bowed and said, 'Good mother, I am a homeless wanderer looking for a place to stay. I will work for my food,' he added hastily.

'Will you, now? I warn you, there is no one here but me.'

'Then you surely could use my help!'

'So…and so…' The old woman circled him, studying him like a hawk studying a mouse. 'Can you work? Are you afraid to get dirty?'

'Yes, good mother. And no, good mother.'

'Very well, then!' She stopped short, hands on hips. 'There is the stable. In it you will find two horses, one black, one white, and you shall take care of them. But I warn you: the white horse is a nasty one! He will bite or kick if you let him. So feed him just enough to keep him alive, and beat him if he so much as snorts at you. But the black horse…ah, pamper him with good food and much grooming.'

'I will do as you ask,' Petit Jean said. To his surprise and delight, the old woman ushered him into the tower. If it was dusty in there, if there were so many spider webs they looked like curtains, well, there was food, too, hot stew in an iron cauldron. Petit Jean ate his fill in the small, cosy kitchen and began to think that his first fears had been silly. This was surely nothing worse than a lonely old woman who was the last of her family.

Nor did he change his mind when she showed him around the tower, through room after room of elegant furniture, all of it in need of dusting. Of course! She had no servants, poor thing!

'Stop,' the old woman said. 'Here are the keys to the tower. You may go wherever it suits you when you aren't tending the horses. One room only is forbidden to you.' She pointed to a tiny door set under a stairway. 'Do not go in there. If you do, you shall regret it, mark my words, boy.'

'Don't worry, good mother,' Petit Jean told her. 'I will not disobey.'

She took him back to the kitchen, and there Petit Jean curled up for the night, and slept without a single dream.

In the morning, the old woman woke him with a shake. 'I will be gone for a week. I have business in the outside world.'

Petit Jean scrambled to his feet. 'Shall I make ready one of the horses?'

'No need. Just be sure to tend them while I am gone.'

With that, the old woman wrapped her cloak about herself — and vanished with a loud bang and a cloud of smoke. A witch! The old woman was a witch!

But she had not harmed him. Besides, Petit Jean told himself, if he ran away, a witch would surely catch him again.

So he went down to the stable to take care of the horses. Sure enough, there they were, a black horse and a white. The white horse didn't look dangerous. In fact, he looked downright sad, head down and ears drooping. Petit Jean, remembering what he had been told, gave the white horse some straw and a little water. But when he began to pick up a stick, the white horse straightened.

'Please don't beat me!'

Petit Jean dropped the stick and nearly dropped himself as well. 'You can talk!'

The white horse looked just as surprised. 'Yes, I can! How amazing! I never even guessed it till this very moment. But what a fortunate thing to discover just now — because we are both in great danger!'

'But the — the old woman said that you were dangerous.'

'Of course she did! She doesn't want you helping me. And she certainly doesn't

46

47

want me helping you! Well now, no need for fear just yet. We have a week. And with your help, I will get back my strength. Feed me well and groom me well. Yes, and don't feed the black horse very well at all! And at the end of the week, you and I will escape!'

The week passed quickly. Every day, Petit Jean fed the white horse and groomed him, and every night, Petit Jean explored the tower, finding room after room. Some had tables and chairs of gleaming wood, dark as night. Others were lined in rich red velvet. Everything, though, was covered with dust. But every night, he refused to even think about that one little door.

On the last day before the witch was to return, however, Petit Jean found himself standing before the little door once more. 'I wonder…do any of these keys fit the lock?'

The smallest key fitted the lock perfectly. Petit Jean hesitated, remembering the witch's warning. But surely it wouldn't hurt to just take the tiniest look inside?

Inside were only a dark room and a narrow ladder leading downwards.

'I wonder where that leads. To a dungeon full of prisoners? Or to treasure?'

Petit Jean tried to leave. But now he was far, far too curious. So he climbed down the ladder, rung by rung, down to a small pool there in the darkness.

'Is this all there is?'

Disappointed, Petit Jean leaned over to see if there was anything under the water. The ends of his hair touched the surface —

And suddenly all Petit Jean's hair was turned to blazing gold!

'No wonder the witch didn't want me to know about this!'

He dipped his few coins into the water — and they, too, came out solid gold.

'What will the witch say if she sees my golden hair? I must wash the gold away!'

But the gold wouldn't wash away. Sadly, Petit Jean went to the white horse for help.

The white horse snorted. 'I can guess where you've been. And no, the gold won't wash out. Go and cut a piece of sheepskin and wear it as a wig.'

'But that won't fool the witch!'

'Not for long. But then, we weren't going to stay here for long, either! So now, here's what we shall do. Give me oats and water. Then bridle and saddle me. Ah yes, and then take that comb and bottle off the tack shelf. I suspect we may find them useful later. One thing more, Petit Jean: take up that stick with which the witch used to beat me. Break it in half. Yes, now, when we are to escape, cross those two pieces in front of you and say, 'Only by road!' Now, hurry out there! She'll be back at any moment!'

Sure enough, no sooner had Petit Jean left the stable than the witch appeared with a swirl of smoke and a roar of thunder.

'H-hello, good mother,' Petit Jean began, trying not to shake. 'Did you — ?'

'What's wrong with your head?' the witch interrupted sharply.

'This? Oh, this is nothing. My head was chilly, so I — I made a hat of this bit of sheepskin.'

The witch snatched it off. Instantly, Petit Jean's golden hair blazed forth. 'I thought as much!' the witch cried. 'You were in the forbidden room! Now you shall pay for that sin with your life!'

Petit Jean snatched up the two halves of the broken stick and crossed them in front of him. 'Only by road!' he cried and ran.

The white horse was waiting. Petit Jean scrambled up into the saddle and away they raced.

'Black horse!' the witch ordered. 'To me!'

Off she rode in pursuit. But the black horse was weakened by poor food and could not run at top speed. Even so it was faster than the white horse, and began to gain on it bit by bit.

'Throw my bridle behind us!' the white horse ordered.

Petit Jean threw the bridle behind them. At once, it changed into a huge mound of bridles, blocking the path from side to side. The witch had to stop to untangle herself and her horse.

'Run on, run on!' Petit Jean urged the white horse.

But all too soon the witch and the black horse were free, and racing after Petit Jean and the white horse again. They began to gain.

'Throw the comb behind us!' the white horse cried.

Petit Jean threw the comb behind them. At once, it changed into a huge mound of combs, blocking the path from side to side. The witch had to stop before the sharp teeth of all those combs stabbed her and her horse.

'Run on, run on!' Petit Jean urged the white horse.

But all too soon, the witch and the black horse were free, and racing after Petit Jean and the white horse again. They began to gain.

'This is our last chance!' the white horse cried. 'Throw the bottle behind us!'

Petit Jean threw the bottle behind them. At once, it changed into a huge mound of bottles, blocking the path from here to there to here again. The witch spurred on her black horse, and it began to climb the mound. But the bottles slipped and slid, and so did the horse. And so did the witch with the horse — and soon witch and horse were covered in a mound of bottles.

'Run on, run on!' Petit Jean cried.

The white horse ran on, but no one followed. He slowed from a gallop to a trot, from a trot to a walk. And at last the white horse stopped.

'That's that,' he said to Petit Jean. 'We are free. Now what shall we do?'

Petit Jean thought. They were free, and the wide, wild world was before them. It no longer seemed so terrible now that he had a friend with him. 'What shall we do? Why, whatever we will!' he exclaimed.

Albania

Horses of the
Mountains and Plains

Albania is a rugged and mountainous country located in the Balkan Peninsula, near Greece and Macedonia, across the Adriatic Sea from Italy. It is home to two distinct kinds of horse, both of them the size of ponies. The mountain horse is the smaller of the two, standing at about 12.2 to 13.2 hands. The plains horse, which is known as the Myszeqea, is a bit bigger, and stands at an average of 13.2 hands.

No one knows when horses first came to Albania, but we do know that the first people who lived in this country were the Illyrians. Illyria was a country to the north of the Adriatic Sea; some Illyrians settled in the northwest part of present-day Albania in the fifth century BC. They will almost certainly have made their way to Albania on horseback. In the centuries that followed, the Albanians gained a reputation as superb riders, and their knights were renowned for their courage on the battlefield.

When Albania became part of the Ottoman Empire, many Arab horses were introduced to Albania and were crossbred with the native breeds. The mountain and plains horses were also crossbred between each other. This crossbreeding led to a finer kind of horse. Nowadays, the typical Albanian horse is noted for its fluid and graceful movements, its agility on difficult terrain, its resistance to disease and its stamina — Albanian horses can undertake long journeys across difficult country without tiring. They are most often used as carriage horses, and for riding and light draught work; however, they are too small to take on heavy agricultural tasks, so in recent decades Haflinger horses have been brought in from Austria to crossbreed with Albanian mountain horses and create a bigger, stronger animal that is better able to help farmers in the hilly regions of the country.

Gjelosh, the hero of the next story, has to undertake a series of difficult challenges, the final one being a journey to the land of the dead. This would not be possible without a loyal, strong and fearless horse. All of these are typical characteristics of the Albanian horse, and they are also the distinctive characteristics of Mingo, the small grey-dun horse who helps Gjelosh to fulfil each of his assignments. Like many fairy tale horses, Mingo is also gifted with the ability to speak the same language as humans, and he is the one on whom Gjelosh depends in finding his bride.

The Boy Who Rode
to the Land of the Dead
Albanian

On a certain day, in a certain year, a boy was born to a poor widow. She named him Gjelosh. All alone Gjelosh grew, all alone he played. He always wondered about his father.

At last his mother told Gjelosh, 'Your father was as he was, no more, no less. He was a hunter, no good it brought him.'

'Then I shall be a hunter, too,' Gjelosh decided, 'and much good will it bring me.'

Off he went into the forest with his father's old rifle. And what should he hear but the yelping of wolves? And what should he find but a little grey-dun horse trapped in a thorny thicket and ringed round by those wolves? Gjelosh fired a shot, and the wolves fled. He released the little horse from the thorny thicket, saying, 'A narrow escape, my friend!'

To his amazement, the little horse replied, 'Friend, indeed! You have saved my life!'

'You — you can talk! How can this be?'

The little horse shook his mane and flicked his tail.

'Only once in a hundred years is a talking horse born, and I am the talking horse for this hundred years. My name,' the little horse added, 'is Mingo. If you will treat me kindly and not as a master treats a slave — yes, and not tell anyone that I can talk — we shall be friends for ever.'

Gjelosh laughed and hugged the little horse. 'We shall be friends, indeed.'

One day, as they hunted together, the little horse said, 'Look what I've found!'

He showed Gjelosh two glittering-bright stones, hidden among the roots of a tree.

'What pretty things!' Gjelosh said. 'I'll take them home to please my mother.'

Alas, what neither he nor Mingo knew was that the king's governor was spying on them. Now, the king of that land was a young man, not a bad man, but not yet quite as wise as he might be. He did not know his own governor was dishonest. The governor stole the two glittering-bright stones from Gjelosh's room and gave them to the king, saying, 'I found these for you, Sire!'

But the young king, being not yet quite as wise as he might be, snapped, 'Only two? That is a miserly gift! I wish enough of the glittering-bright stones to build me a palace!'

The governor had no idea where so many stones could be found. But he didn't dare tell that to the king! So off he hurried to Gjelosh. 'The king orders you to find enough glittering-bright stones to build him a palace! If you do not obey his wish,' the governor added sternly, 'you shall be put to death!'

Once the governor had ridden off, Mingo said, 'Do not fear, Gjelosh. I can show you enough glittering-bright stones to build a dozen palaces. In the mountains lies a hoard of the stones, guarded by the one-eyed donkey, Beiram.'

'But no man can kill Beiram!' Gjelosh cried.

'Ah, but we horses know the secret to Beiram's life, and it is this: it lies in his single eye. Only the kick from a horse's hoof may destroy that eye.'

'But Beiram might kill you!'

'Don't worry for me, my friend! All will be well.'

Gjelosh rode Mingo up into the mountains, and hid. With a terrible scream, Beiram appeared, a gigantic donkey red as blood, his one eye blazing with flame. He charged Mingo — but the little horse dodged and darted, nipped and neighed, then galloped round and round again, till Beiram was so dizzy he crashed down on his knees. With one mighty kick, Mingo struck Beiram's eye — and the donkey fell down dead.

'There!' Mingo said. 'I told you that all would be well. Come, let us take these glittering-bright stones to the king.'

This was not what the governor had planned. He had wanted to give the stones to the king himself, and take all the praise. Now he had to watch the king praise Gjelosh instead!

'You will stay here at court,' the king exclaimed. 'I like having clever men about me.'

The palace of the glittering-bright stones was built, and people from throughout the land came to admire it. And when they learned that it was Gjelosh who'd brought the glittering-bright stones, they admired him as well!

'This is bad,' the governor muttered angrily. 'This is terrible. This is not to be endured! Gjelosh must be destroyed!'

So the governor went to the king. Smoothly, he said, 'Sire, you are surely the greatest monarch in all the world! Have you not built the most splendid of palaces? It is...so sad.' He pretended to wipe away a tear.

'What is sad?' the king asked.

'Alas, alas, that the late king, your royal father, does not know of his son's splendour!'

The young king sighed. 'That is sad, indeed. I do wish that my father could know.'

'But — wait! He can know! You can send him a letter!'

'To the Land Where the Dead Live? Can a living man go there?'

'Only a very clever man, the cleverest man in all the land. Only Gjelosh could do it.'

'Have him brought to me!' the king cried. He wrote a letter to his dead father. When Gjelosh stood before him, the king said, 'You shall take this letter to my father in the Land Where the Dead Live.'

'B-but how can a living man go there? Yes, and how can he return alive?'

'That is for you to learn! Now, go, and if you fail, I shall order you slain!'

Gjelosh, weeping, wandered off to the stables to find Mingo.

Why do you weep, my friend?' Mingo asked.

'The king has ordered me to deliver a letter to the Land Where the Dead Live. But it is surely the governor who speaks behind him. The governor has long envied me — and now he means my death!'

'Wait, wait,' Mingo said soothingly. 'Let us go ask the Thopch for advice.'

The Thopch was a mountain dwarf, a being of great wisdom. Mingo and Gjelosh waited until precisely the stroke of noon. Then a mountain cave opened with a roar of thunder, and the Thopch came out. He was so short, he barely reached Gjelosh's knee. The Thopch's ears were so large they wrapped about his head like a turban, and his white beard was so long it wrapped about his body like a coat.

'We seek your wisdom, O Thopch,' Mingo said.

'There has long been friendship between the horse-kind and me. Ask what you would.'

So Mingo told him of the letter to be delivered to the Land Where the Dead Live. The Thopch shut his eyes and pondered the problem for a full hour. Then he opened them again and shook his head. 'There is only one who may solve this problem, and that is Beautiful-of-the-Earth. But she is the prisoner of a Dif.'

Now, a Dif was both giant and demon, huge and cruel. When a Dif found a

woman alone, he would carry her off to be his slave, to shoo the flies away from him when he slept. When a Dif found a man alone, the Dif tore him apart and ate him. Gjelosh hung his head in despair, but Mingo nudged him with a soft muzzle.

'Don't give up, my friend! Good Thopch, where does this Dif live?'

'On the mountain that lies west of here, the mountain with its feet in a swamp and its head in the clouds. If you would live, do not go there save in the few hours between noon and sunset. That is when the Dif leaves his mountain to go hunting.'

'Then we have only to wait,' Gjelosh said, 'and steal away Beautiful-of-the-Earth!'

'Not so fast! When the Dif leaves, he changes Beautiful-of-the-Earth into something else. The only hope you have of recognising her is this: he may only turn her into an object once. Each time he must find another shape for her. By now, he must have run out of such ordinary things as trees or rocks.'

'Then all we must do,' Mingo said, 'is look for something that doesn't belong on a mountain!'

Off Gjelosh and Mingo went to the Dif's mountain. They hid, waiting carefully until the hours between noon and sunset, and saw the Dif storm off in the form of a huge, swirling, dark thundercloud. Hastily, knowing that they had only a few short hours in which to search, they climbed the mountain, hunting for something that didn't belong on a mountain. Trees? No, they belonged. Rocks? They certainly belonged! Bushes? Birds? What, oh, what? All that afternoon, Gjelosh and Mingo searched, as the sun moved ever closer to the horizon.

Then, just before it set, Gjelosh said, 'What is hanging from that tree?'

'A haunch of smoked meat!' Mingo exclaimed. 'No one would leave smoked meat hanging from a tree halfway up a Dif's mountain! That can only be Beautiful-of-the-Earth. Climb up there and touch her. The disguise will break.'

So Gjelosh climbed the tree and touched the smoked meat — and instantly the spell shattered, and he found himself staring at a young woman so lovely his heart nearly stopped for wonder.

'You aren't the Dif!' she cried in relief. 'You are the first man I've seen since the Dif caught me many years ago. I beg you, take me away from here — I shall be

58

your wife or even your slave! Just hurry, because the sun is almost setting, and the Dif will return and eat you!'

'I don't keep slaves,' Gjelosh told her, 'and I don't know if I will live long enough to woo you. But the Dif shall have you no longer.'

They climbed down from the tree, and Gjelosh set her on the saddle behind him. A great, cold wind suddenly swept down the mountain, and the earth shook.

'The Dif is returning!' Beautiful-of-the-Earth cried.

'Run!' Gjelosh shouted to Mingo.

Mingo ran faster than the wind itself. He ran through the night right into the dawn. Only then did he stop to rest.

'We're safe now,' he panted.

'You've saved me,' Beautiful-of-the-Earth said. 'What may I offer in return?'

'Some of your wisdom,' Gjelosh said. He told her about the royal command, how he must take the letter to the Land Where the Dead Live, and how it was all part of the governor's wicked plot to be rid of him.

Beautiful-of-the-Earth smiled. 'Why, that is a problem easily solved! Can you write?'

'No,' Gjelosh admitted. Of course, neither could Mingo.

'No matter,' Beautiful-of-the-Earth said. 'Take me to where there is parchment and ink.'

She wrote a letter, an answer from the live king's dead father. And in it, she said:

'My son, I have read your letter with much joy at learning how splendidly you rule.

I tell you that I rule almost as splendidly here. I only lack one thing, the wisdom of your governor. Pray, send him to me without delay, and put in his place he who gives you this letter.'

Gjelosh waited, hidden, for many days, as long as it might take a man to ride to and back from the Land Where the Dead Live. While he waited, he and Beautiful-of-the-Earth courted each other, and fell in love.

At last, Gjelosh put on the most ragged clothes he could find, and left Mingo's coat ungroomed. Taking the letter, he set out for court like a man who has undergone a terrible ordeal. Mingo staggered like a horse who had run for his life.

'Here is what you told me to bring,' Gjelosh told the young king, handing over the letter.

The king read, and was overjoyed. The governor watched, and was consumed with rage. What, had Gjelosh truly returned? Had he really brought back a letter from the Land Where the Dead Live?

'This man is a liar!' the governor roared. 'The letter is a forgery! He has no more been to the Land Where the Dead Live than have I!' So furious was the governor that Gjelosh had returned, he forgot all wisdom. He burst out, 'No one can go there but — but the dead themselves!'

The king frowned at him. 'Yet you told me to send Gjelosh there. Are you mocking me?'

'No, Sire! Never!'

'Have you been mocking me all along? If you did bid me send Gjelosh where no living man may go, then indeed, you did mock me! My father asks for you. Get you gone to him — or I shall hang you here and now!'

The governor fled, and the king made Gjelosh governor in his place. Gjelosh wed Beautiful-of-the-Earth, and governed wisely with her. And he and Mingo remained dearest friends for all the days of their lives.

Iran

The
Caspian Horse

*T*he people of Iran have an ancient saying: 'When our children are between the ages of seven and seventeen, we teach them two lessons: how to tell the truth, and how to ride.' So it is no surprise that horse riding has been a central part of Iranian culture for many centuries. In fact, the history of horses in Iran reaches right back to the third millennium BC.

Iran used to be known as Persia. The breed that is unique to this region is the Caspian, which is probably the most ancient domestic breed of horse in existence. The Caspian horse is represented in carvings at the ancient capital of the Persian Empire, Persepolis, and it also appears on the seal of King Darius, who ruled Persia in the sixth century BC. This regal breed is quite exquisite — it has a delicate head and a dished face, like that of an Arab horse, with large, prominent eyes, flaring nostrils, and a silky mane and tail. It is very spirited, with a proud bearing, and seems almost to float as it moves, with its head and tail held high. Yet it stands just 10 to 12 hands high, making it smaller than the average modern-day pony!

Caspian horses disappeared from history when the Muslims conquered Persia in AD 627. Until 1965, everyone believed that they were extinct. Then an American woman, Louise Firouz, who ran a riding school for children in Tehran, heard rumours of a wild herd of miniature horses in the remote Elburz mountains in northern Iran, near the Caspian Sea. She set out on horseback to track them down — and found her way to a scattered group of about thirty small horses which she immediately recognised as Caspians. She brought back thirteen of the horses, and blood tests proved her belief that they belonged to the ancestral breed from which Arabian and other hot-blooded horses are all descended.

The Iran–Iraq war and other political upheavals in the Middle East threatened the newly rediscovered Caspian with extinction in the later decades of the twentieth century. However, a number were exported and today about three hundred survive worldwide, mainly in England, France, Australia, New Zealand and the United States.

The colt Qeytas, who stars in the next story, is not only an extraordinary jumper like most Caspians — he can also fly! Qeytas saves his royal master from being murdered, and makes sure that he finds his way to a successful and happy new life.

The Colt Qeytas
Iranian

Once upon a time, there was a king with only one son. The king's wife had died, and so he married again to give the young prince a mother. But the new queen hated the young prince. She wanted her own children to inherit the throne!

The prince had a friend, a magical talking colt named Qeytas. When the prince was off with the mullah, the priest who taught him, the queen slipped poison into his food. But Qeytas saw this and warned the prince, 'Do not eat.'

'I am not hungry,' the prince told the queen.

The queen frowned. But she watched the path the prince used when he went off to the mullah. She had a secret pit dug, and covered the opening with leaves.

But Qeytas saw this, and warned the prince, 'There is a pit in your path.'

So the prince tiptoed carefully around it.

The queen frowned. 'It is the colt Qeytas who protects him. Remove the colt, and the prince will be without a friend.'

She took to her bed, weeping. 'Only a soup made of the colt Qeytas will cure me!'

The prince said to his father, 'What must be, must be. Only let me ride Qeytas one last time.'

He put on his jewels and his royal robes, and rode Qeytas once around the palace, twice around the palace, and as they rode a third time around the palace, Qeytas leapt up into the air and flew off. No one in that land saw the prince or the colt again.

On they flew, over hills and plains, till at last they came to a town. Qeytas landed near the royal gardens and said, 'Here is where you shall find your new life. First give

me your jewels and royal robes. Disguise yourself in dirty old clothes and cover your head with that scrap of sheepskin. It is not yet time for you to be recognised. You must find yourself work in the royal gardens.'

'I will do that,' the prince said. 'But what about you?'

Qeytas shook his shining mane. 'Pull some hairs from my mane and keep them safe. Whenever you need me, you need only burn a hair, and I shall appear.'

With that, Qeytas flew off. The prince found himself a job in the royal gardens, and worked long and hard for days. But he was lonely, and one night he burned a hair of Qeytas' mane. Instantly, the colt was there with him, and the prince put on his royal clothes again and rode Qeytas.

The king's youngest daughter was on her balcony, and she saw the prince. Not with one heart but a hundred hearts did she fall in love with him, and she went hurrying down from the palace to see who this stranger might be. But by the time

she reached the garden, Qeytas had flown away, and only the gardener's boy with his scrap of sheepskin was there. The princess was not fooled. She studied him, then said, 'Aha! I know you even under that disguise.' Snatching the sheepskin from his head, she demanded, 'Tell me who you are.'

The prince had fallen just as suddenly and surely in love, and he told her his story. 'Keep my secret,' he pleaded. And the princess agreed.

The princess had two older sisters. And the king's wazir, his prime minister, was ambitious. He wanted to marry his two sons to the king's two older daughters. So he made sure his sons secretly courted the two older daughters.

Then he went to the king with three lovely melons, and begged the king to cut them open, saying, 'This is a riddle, Your Majesty.'

The king cut the melons open. The largest melon was very ripe, the middle melon was ripe, but the third melon was barely ripe. The king frowned. 'What is the answer?'

'These are your daughters, Your Majesty. The eldest and middle daughters are ripe for marriage. The third is still a child.'

'True,' the king mused. 'What do you think I should do?'

'Invite the court to a great feast. Give the princesses each a golden orange. As each princess sees the man whom she is willing to wed, she must hand him her orange.'

The king did as the wazir bid. The two older princesses handed their oranges to the sons of the wazir. But the youngest princess refused all the glittering nobles. She hunted for the dirty, ragged gardener's boy with his sheepskin on his head, and gave him her orange. Everyone in the court made fun of her.

The king gave his oldest daughters in marriage to the sons of the wazir. But the thought of his youngest daughter's choice of the gardener's boy made him ill with grief. So ill, that he took to his bed. The royal doctors treated him with different medicines, but nothing helped.

At last a wise man said, 'There is a golden bird in the desert beyond the desert, and no one yet has been able to catch it. If any were to kill that bird and give it to the king to eat, he would be cured.'

'We will bring back the golden bird for the king,' cried the two sons of the wazir.

'I will go with you,' said the gardener's boy.

The wazir's sons laughed. 'What nonsense is this? We are the sons of a nobleman — while you are barely a human being!'

'I will go with you,' the gardener's boy insisted.

When they saw that he would not give up, the sons of the wazir said to the royal groom, 'Find him the worst nag in all the stables.'

Then they dressed in their noble finery and mounted the finest of horses. Together with servants and guards, they rode off on their quest.

The prince rode after them on his slow, limping nag. When they had left him far behind, he stopped and burned a hair of Qeytas' mane.

Instantly, Qeytas appeared. 'All you need to cure the king,' he said, 'is the golden bird's head and feet. And that, we shall win.'

The prince changed into his royal robes and sprang on to Qeytas. Off they flew, and soon came upon the two sons of the wazir, who were trying and trying to catch the golden bird, but missing it each time.

'Who are you?' they asked the prince.

'I am a king's son, out seeing the world. What are you trying to do?'

'We must bring back that golden bird to our king, our father-in-law, so that he may eat it and be well again. But we cannot catch that cursed bird!'

'I can,' the prince told them. 'If you will sign a paper saying that you will be my slaves, I will catch the golden bird for you.'

The two sons of the wazir whispered together. 'He doesn't know who we are. How can he make us his slaves? We'll take the bird and hurry home, and be heroes.'

So they willingly signed the paper. The prince leapt on to Qeytas' back, Qeytas leapt into the air, and in no time at all, they had hunted down and slain the golden bird. Keeping the head and feet for himself, the prince handed over the rest to the two sons of the wazir. Delighted to have outwitted this stranger, they galloped away.

Qeytas carried the prince back to where he'd left the lame old nag. Changing back

into his gardener's boy's rags, the prince waved goodbye to Qeytas and started slowly back to the palace. The two sons of the wazir quickly overtook him, sneering at him as they galloped past. As soon as they reached the royal palace, they cooked the golden bird in a fine sauce, put it in a golden bowl, and brought it to the king with a golden spoon.

The king ate, but he became even more ill.

The gardener's boy cooked the head and feet of the golden bird, put them in a wooden bowl, and brought it to the king with a wooden spoon.

'What mockery is this?' the king shouted.

But his wife murmured, 'The poor boy has travelled long and hard. It would be unkind not at least to taste his offering.'

The king took a taste. Then he took another taste. Soon he had eaten it all and leapt out of bed, completely healthy once more. 'Send for my sons-in-law!' he ordered.

When the two sons of the wazir appeared, the king roared at them, 'What was good, you gave away to this poor boy. What was bad, you fed to me!'

'But we gave nothing to this boy!' they argued. 'He couldn't keep up with us at all!'

'My poor old nag could not,' the gardener's boy agreed. 'I got what I got from a prince. Ask these two, Your Majesty, ask them what befell them with that prince.'

And with their heads lowered, the two sons told how they had signed the deed of slavery, and how the stranger had then slain the golden bird and taken only its head and feet. 'He must have given them to this poor boy.'

The gardener's boy smiled and pulled a paper out of his clothing. 'I was that stranger. Here is the deed of slavery they signed.' He pulled off the sheepskin and threw off the rags, and there stood the prince in his royal robes.

The king was overjoyed. 'My daughter was right and I was wrong! You two shall be wed at once.'

In time, the prince and his princess came to sit on the royal throne. The prince set free his two brothers-in-law, and made them his wazirs.

And what of the colt Qeytas? He flew free wherever he wished. But he returned whenever he wished.

Hungary

Horses of
the Puszta

*H*ungary is a country that has always been famous for its horses. In fact, the very first Hungarians, the Magyars, were great warriors who rode their horses through the steppes of central Asia and settled in Hungary during the ninth century AD. These Magyars eventually became one of the first peoples of the world to breed horses.

Over the years, the Magyars developed a prosperous rural economy that had at its centre the breeding of huge herds of cattle, which roamed across the Great Plain, or Puszta. In many ways, this vast expanse of land is still unchanged even today, with acre after acre of open grassland interspersed with fields of bright red paprika. This beautiful, windswept landscape is punctuated only by whitewashed farmhouses, thatched roadside inns, and thriving stud farms. The land is fertile, but the people and animals who live there have to endure long, hard winters and hot summers. To tend their cattle herds, they need horses that are small and fast, with a lot of stamina.

The most notable riders in Hungary were and still are the cowboys of the Puszta. Known locally as *csikós*, Hungarian cowboys are renowned for their great riding skills. The most spectacular demonstration of their horsemanship is a dramatic feat called the 'Puszta Five' in which a *csikó* stands in the middle of five horses — three in front and two in back — and steers them wherever he wants using especially long reins.

In recent centuries, Hungarians have developed three breeds in particular: the Nonius is an all-round horse which evolved in the nineteenth century and was used for drawing carriages as well as for riding. The Furioso is closely related to the Nonius, but is more refined, and powerful enough to race at an international level in steeplechases. But the most famous Hungarian horse is the Shagya Arab, a cross between Hungary's native Babolna horses and the Arab horses of the desert. It is more robust than a pure-bred Arab, and is usually grey in colour, with a gentle, intelligent nature. Shagya Arabs have been used as cavalry mounts and carriage horses as well as for light draft work. Today, they are still in great demand in Germany and the United States as well as the countries of Eastern Europe.

The Taltos horse in this story could be any one of these breeds — but as a creature with quite unusual magical powers, perhaps he is a breed all of his own!

The Taltos Horse
Hungarian

Once upon a time, in a land beyond beyond, there was an old king with three sons. Now, there was a strangeness about that old king: with one eye, he constantly wept, but with the other, he laughed. His sons wondered about this, and at last the oldest son went to his father and asked, 'Why is it that you weep with one eye and laugh with the other?'

The king snatched up a little dagger and threw it at his son. The oldest son fled the room.

Now it was the turn of the middle son. 'Father, why is it that you weep with one eye and laugh with the other?'

The king snatched up his little dagger and threw it at his son. The middle son fled the room.

And now it was the turn of the youngest son, Marko. 'Good day to you, Father. Why is it that you weep with one eye and laugh with the other?'

The king snatched up his little dagger and threw it at his son. Marko didn't move, trusting his father. Sure enough, the dagger flew by him without touching so much as a hair on his head, and fell harmlessly to the floor.

'You are truly my son,' the king said. 'The reason I both weep and laugh is that I think of my dearest friend who has gone I know not where. If I could but see him again, both my eyes would first weep, then laugh with joy.'

Marko told this to his brothers.

'I will find my father's friend,' the oldest brother said, and set out on the road.

He travelled on for two months until he came to a narrow bridge made of bright copper plates. The bridge swayed in the wind, and the oldest son did not dare to cross it. Instead, he broke off a copper plate to show his father how far he had ridden.

But the king shook his head in disgust. 'Two months to ride that far? When I was your age, I rode that distance in a day!'

So now it was the middle brother who rode out. After two months, he came to the copper bridge. He, too, was afraid to cross. But he dismounted, and led his horse across, then rode on for two more months. Soon he came to a bridge of shining silver plates, chiming like little bells in the wind. Afraid that someone might hear and attack him if he crossed that noisy bridge, the middle son broke off a little silver plate and rode home.

But the king shook his head in disgust. 'Four months to ride that far? When I was your age, I rode that distance in two days!'

So now it was Marko's turn. His brothers laughed at him. 'Do you think you can do what we could not?'

'I will do what I can for our father's sake,' Marko said simply, and went on to the stables.

But before he could reach them, the skinniest, ugliest, oldest horse Marko had ever seen came staggering up to him. 'You don't want any of the horses in there. You want me.'

When Marko heard the horse speak, he drew back in wonder. This could only be a taltos horse! 'What do you need from me? Oats? Hay?'

'First bring me a bag of barley.' Marko did, and the old horse swallowed the barley in one gulp.

'Now bring me a bag of millet grain.'

Marko did, and the old horse swallowed the millet grain in one gulp.

'Now bring me a bag of charcoal.'

'Charcoal!' Marko exclaimed. But he did as the old horse bade. The old horse swallowed the charcoal in one gulp.

'Now give me a good grooming,' he ordered.

Marko groomed him from forelock to tail. Wonder of wonders, once he was done, the skinny old horse was now a shining horse of power, his coat gleaming gold, his mane and tail shimmering silver. A taltos horse, indeed!

But in the next moment, he changed into a skinny old horse again. 'Now,' the taltos horse told Marko, 'you must ask your father for the sword and saddle he used in his youth, when he and his friend rode together.'

The king was delighted when Marko asked for the sword and saddle. 'You, at least, are trying to help me!'

His two brothers laughed at the sight of Marko riding off on a skinny old horse. But as soon as they were out of sight, the horse became the beautiful taltos steed again.

'Close your eyes tight, Marko,' he warned.

Marko obeyed, and felt a mighty wind nearly sweep him from the saddle.

'Open your eyes again,' the horse told him.

They were at the copper bridge. It had taken the oldest son two months to go this far; it had taken the taltos horse only a few moments.

'Now you must cut off my head,' the horse said. 'Don't worry: in my right ear is a vial of magic water. Sprinkle it on me and I will come alive again. But before you can revive me, you must fight the Dragon of the Copper Bridge. Let him challenge you four times before you accept, then throw your sword at him.'

Marko, weeping, cut off the head of the taltos horse. And sure enough, up rose the dragon, a terrible six-headed monster with flaming eyes and gleaming fangs. Marko's heart sank at the sight of him, but he waited. The dragon shouted, 'Come and fight me, little man!'

'Not yet,' Marko told him. 'First I must re-buckle my sword belt.'

'Come and fight me!' the dragon shouted.

'Not yet. My sword belt does not hang right.'

'Come and fight me, I say!'

'Not yet. I must draw my sword.'

'For the fourth and last time, fight me or I will kill you where you stand!'

'Now I will fight,' Marko said, and with all his might he hurled his sword at the dragon. It cut off all six heads at a blow, and the dragon fell dead.

Marko quickly sprinkled the magic water on the taltos horse, and the horse sprang up alive again. 'Well done, Marko! Now, get on my back and shut your eyes.'

A mighty wind nearly swept Marko from the saddle. When he opened his eyes, he found that they had reached the silver bridge.

'Now you must cut off my head,' the taltos horse told him, 'and take the vial of magic water from my right ear. Then you must fight the Dragon of the Silver Bridge. Let him challenge you four times, then throw your sword at him.'

So Marko cut off the head of the taltos horse, and soon the Dragon of the Silver Bridge appeared. He was even more terrible than his brother, with twelve hideous heads and fiery eyes. But Marko waited till the dragon had challenged him once, twice, thrice, four times, then threw his sword. Sure enough, swift as lightning, the sword cut through all twelve heads, and the dragon fell dead.

Marko sprinkled the magic water over the horse, and the taltos horse sprang up alive once more. 'Well done, Marko! But we still have a way to go. On to my back, Marko, and keep your eyes shut!'

Once again, they raced like the wind, and this time came to a great bridge of black iron. 'Here you must face the Dragon of the Iron Bridge,' the taltos horse warned. 'First, cut off my head as before, and take the vial of magic water from my right ear. Then do all as you did before, and have no fear.'

It was not easy to have no fear when Marko saw the Dragon of the Iron Bridge. For this dragon had no less than twenty-four heads, and each head had terrible fiery eyes and terrible clashing fangs. But Marko obeyed the taltos horse and cut off his head. Then he let the dragon challenge him four times, and hurled his sword at it. Straight and true, the sword cut off those twenty-four terrible heads, and the dragon fell dead.

Quickly, Marko sprinkled the magic water on the taltos horse, and the horse sprang up alive. 'Well done, Marko! Now we must ride on over the Glass Mountain. But have no fear: my horseshoes are studded with diamond spikes, and will not slip. Keep your eyes closed, though: the brightness of the glass could dazzle you.'

This time Marko could not resist it. He opened his eyes the tiniest bit. Ah, but the dazzling glass was so bright that he quickly shut his eyes again.

'We are safely past,' the taltos horse said. 'Open your eyes and tell me what you see.'

'Darkness!' Marko cried.

'That is the Land of the Demons. But have no fear. We aren't going there.'

The taltos horse brought Marko to a meadow bright with green grass waving like the smooth waves of the sea in a sweet breeze. In the middle of the meadow stood a silken tent, and beside that tent was a shining horse. 'Brother!' he whinnied.

'Brother!' the taltos horse whinnied back.

Within the tent, a man who looked to be the same age as Marko's father lay sleeping. As he slept, a gleaming sword patrolled, moving smoothly through the air in a protective circle about him. 'That is the one you seek,' the taltos horse whispered. 'That is your father's friend, and that sword is twin to the one you bear.'

Marko dismounted. The man was sleeping like one who was very weary. 'It would be rude to wake him,' Marko thought, and sat down. But he, too, was very weary, and soon enough, he, too, fell asleep.

When he woke, the man was watching him. 'You are a polite young man,' the man said. 'You could have awakened me, but you let me rest. Now, what wind has blown you here?'

'No wind, but the taltos horse who is a brother to your own. I am Prince Marko, and you and my father were once the dearest of friends.'

Quickly, Marko explained why he had come. The older man cried out in joy, 'I should dearly love to see my friend again! But, alas,' he added more sadly, 'I cannot. I must guard this meadow, the Silk Meadow, against the Land of Demons.'

'Then let us fight the demons,' Marko said. 'Let us defeat them!'

So Marko and the older man gathered an army and rode against the army of the demons. Marko fought here, Marko fought there, and everywhere he struck, he took off a hundred demon heads.

And when the battle was done, why, there were no more demons left in the human world.

'Now I may go with you to see my dear friend,' the older man said.

Marko gave him two diamond-studded horseshoes from his own taltos horse's saddlebag. Now both horse brothers could ride over the Glass Mountain. On they sped together until at last they were back in Marko's father's kingdom.

Soon the king and his oldest, dearest friend were reunited. And much joy was there then!

And what of Marko? Since the oldest and middle sons had failed in their quest, Marko became his father's heir. In time, with the aid of the taltos horse, he ruled the kingdom both wisely and well.

Sources

PAWNEE
The Ocean of Story, 10 vols. — N.M. Penzer, ed., Motilal Banarsidass, 1968.
Pawnee Stories and Folk-tales — George Grinnell, Forest and Stream Publishing Company, 1889.
Tales of the North American Indians — Stith Thompson, Indiana University Press, 1929.

INDIAN
Folk Tales and Fairy Stories from India — Sudhin N. Ghose, The Golden Cockerel Press, 1961.
Folktales of India — Brenda E.F. Beck, et al, The University of Chicago Press, 1981.
The Panchatantra — Arthur W. Ryder, Arthur W., trans., The University of Chicago Press, 1925.

BASQUE
A View from the Witch's Cave — Luis de Barandiaran Irizar, University of Nebraska Press, 1991.
Legendes du Pays Basque, D'apres la Tradition — Jean Barbier, Delgrave, 1931.
Tales of a Basque Grandmother — Frances Carpenter, Doubleday, Doran & Company, 1930.

RUSSIAN
The Firebird — Anonymous trans. Progress Publishers, undated.
The Little Humpbacked Horse — P. Yershov, Progress Publishers, 1957.
Russian Fairy Tales — Aleksandr, Afanas'ev. Pantheon Books, 1945.
Tales of the Amber Sea — Irina Zheleznova, Progress Publishers, 1974.

CANADIAN
Folktales of French Canada — Edith Fowke, NC Press Limited, 1982.
The Golden Phoenix and Other French-Canadian FairyTales — Marius Barbeau and Michael Hornyansky,
Henry Z. Walck, Inc., 1958.
Tales of the North American Indians — Stith Thompson, Indiana University Press, 1929.

ALBANIAN
Albanian Wonder Tales — Post Wheeler, Doubleday, Doran and Company, 1936.
Tricks of Women and Other Albanian Tales — Paul Fenimore Cooper, William Morrow & Company, 1928.

IRANIAN
Persian Fairy Tales — Eleanor Brockett, Frederick Muller, Ltd., 1962.
Persian Tales — D.L.R. and E.O. Lorimer, Macmillan and Company, Ltd., 1919.

HUNGARIAN
Folktales of Hungary — Linda Degh, ed., The University of Chicago Press, 1965.
Hungarian Folk Beliefs — Tekla, Domotor. Indiana University Press, 1981.

GENERAL
Animal Folklore: from Black Cats to White Horses — Edward F. Dolan, Ivy Books, 1992.
The Horse in Magic and Myth — M. Oldfield Howey, Castle Books, 1958.
If You Had a Horse — Margaret Hodges, Charles Scribner's Sons, 1984.
The Magical History of the Horse — Janet & Virginia Russell Farrar, Robert Hale, Ltd., 1992.
Merlin's Kin: World Tales of the Heroic Magician — Josepha Sherman, August House, 1998.
There Was a Horse: Folktales from Many Lands — Phyllis R. Fenner, Alfred A. Knopf, 1941.
Wonder Tales of Horses and Heroes — Frances Carpenter, Doubleday and Company, 1952.